MW00875256

HAPPY DAYZ
THINGS THAT MAKE YOU SMILE
COLORING BOOK

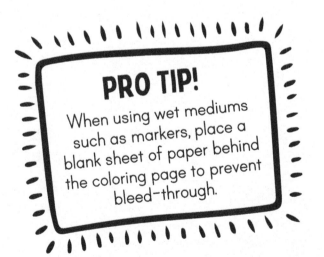

PRO TIP!

When using wet mediums such as markers, place a blank sheet of paper behind the coloring page to prevent bleed-through.

THANK YOU FOR YOUR PURCHASE!

Made in the USA
Las Vegas, NV
18 December 2024

14653153R00050